THE KILLER OF ALPHAS

BY: NORA XHEM

TABLE OF CONTENTS

PROLOGUE:

I woke up with the sharpest pain ever, knowing exactly what it meant. I groaned as I sat up slowly, reaching for the drawer to my right. Opening it carefully, I grabbed the thing I needed.

Getting out of bed didn't help my breathing at all, but I pushed the pain aside as I made my way out of the room and down the stairs, heading straight toward the room at the end of the hallway. The pain became unbearable to the point where I had to stop and take a breath. Still, I forced myself through it.

One hand on the handle, I pushed the door open. Beholding the sight in front of me, I cocked the handgun, finger on the trigger, pointing it at them—my so-called soulmate. They finally noticed me, and that's when the shots were fired.
Blood splattered everywhere, screams filled the room. I smirked as I aimed the gun at him again. Taking one final breath, I released the trigger, killing him on the spot.

"I'm not the one to fool," I said as I turned around and walked away. Walking down the empty hallways, I knew soon enough they would be filled. Of course, they would find the dead body of their precious soon-to-be Alpha. Once they did, I would no longer be here. Everything was perfect. I smirked darkly.

I left before anyone could interrogate me, starting a new life somewhere else.

Punishment for those who dare hurt the Alpha is death—but I don't care.

CHAPTER 1:

Emery

I packed everything I needed for my better life out there. Changing my clothes and shoes, I made sure not to leave any trace of myself behind. Opening the window, I threw the bag out first, then hung one leg over the sill. Taking one final look at my room, I jumped, landing sharp and quiet.

I took off, never to be seen—or at least, I hoped that would be the case. I highly doubted it, since there would most likely be punishment or consequences to face… that is, if I were caught.

I made it to a bus station and bought a one-way ticket to anywhere far from here. Ticket in hand, bag in the other, I sat down on the bench and glanced
at the clock.

11:30 p.m.

I sighed and looked around, realizing I was the only one there. Suddenly, someone sat down—an old man.

"Now, where would a young lady like yourself be traveling to at this hour?" he asked me.

"Oh, uh… just going to visit my aunt. It's her birthday in two days, so I decided to surprise her," I replied with a complete lie. I don't have an aunt.

I mainly grew up with the Alpha and Luna of the pack. I don't know my parents—they dropped me off with them when I was a baby. I guess they

didn't want to be tied down by a child. Then why have one at all? I'm not sure. People are weird.

"I see," he said, glancing at his watch. Suddenly, a bell rang. "Well, that is my cue. Have a safe trip." He tipped his hat and walked off.

"You too," I replied, feeling at ease.

Eventually, it was my turn to board the bus. I took the seat furthest in the back, closed the curtain, and placed my bag beside me as people continued to board.

You may ask how—and why—I am running away. It is quite simple, and it all started last night when I discovered my mate having sex with another female who wasn't his chosen mate, gifted by the Moon Goddess. I always suspected something was going on between them, but I played it off as nothing since it never became physical enough to hurt me—or to make me feel.

That didn't last very long. They decided to take it to a new level. What an idiot… did he forget that anything he does with another female, I feel it too?

I relaxed into the seat, and eventually let the soft hum of the bus lull me to sleep.

CHAPTER 2:

Emery

SCREECH

The loud noise startled me awake as the bus came to an abrupt stop.
The driver yelled, "We have arrived at Orchid Bus Stop."
My stop. Perfect.

I grabbed my stuff, pulled my hood up, and exited the bus.

"Excuse me, how far is the nearest town from here?" I asked the bus
conductor.

"Ten miles to the left of this bus station," she answered.

"Thank you," I said, then turned to the left.

This may take me a while. Better start now.
I nodded in determination and began my journey. Halfway through, I
realized the pain I had felt when Chase was sleeping with her was
gone.

It is said that when two soulmates meet or discover each other, a bond
is created—through mating, of course. But if one of them mates with
another wolf, their mate suffers. And if their mate dies, they also feel
another kind of pain—the pain of losing a loved one.

From the day I turned eighteen and we discovered we were mates, I
knew he didn't want me. Who would want a human? I could feel it
and see it in his eyes. He should've just rejected me. But he didn't,

because of his mother's feelings. She loved—well, loved—me as her own daughter. At least, I suppose she did. I can only hope she did. Not having my own mother has always left a hollow space in my chest and in my life.

I shook the thoughts away as I finally reached the town after a few hours.

At first glance, it was clear this place wasn't small. It was spacious and clean.

Hm. I guess I could make a life here.

I walked further, searching for a motel. Eventually, after getting slightly familiar with the town, I found one. It looked good—clean and proper. I paid for a room and got my key.

ROOM 208.

I stood in front of the door, slid the key in, and turned the knob. Pushing the door open, I felt a strange sense of déjà vu. After switching on the light, I stepped inside, dropped my bag on the floor, and plopped onto the bed.

Kicking off my shoes, I snuggled into the soft sheets until I eventually blacked out.

Later that day, I woke up refreshed. Looking around, I reminded myself I was in a different place. With a sigh, I got up, used the bathroom, washed my face, and changed into a different shirt with a light cardigan. Grabbing my bag, I left the room

I'd best go job hunting; and get dinner too. I'm not sure what kind of life I'll have here, but it's not like I can't make the best of it.
As I walked out of the motel, I noticed a stack of maps near the door. Grabbing one, I began walking. The people, the atmosphere—it was amazing. I felt free and at ease, far away from all the drama. A sign reading *Joe & Mina's Diner* caught my eye, along with a "Help Wanted" sign displayed right up front. I shrugged and walked into the diner. The bell above the door announced my entrance. People glanced my way, then quickly returned to their meals.

"Howdy, I'm Bette. What can I do for you?" asked a woman in her thirties, with brown curly pin-up hair.

"Oh, uh, hi. I saw the sign outside and was wondering if there are any positions available?" I asked nervously.

"Yes, you've come to the right place. Follow me," she said.
I nodded and followed her into the office. She sat down and motioned for me to do the same.

"Alright, all you have to do is fill out this information. We don't ask for much. Training will be paid, and you'll get benefits such as sick days, vacation, medical coverage, etc." she explained.

I nodded. "Do you have a pen?"

She smiled and handed me one. I began filling out the form—date of birth, name, temporary address; careful not to reveal too much. When I finished, I handed it back to her. She scanned it for a few seconds, then set it down in front of her.

"When are you available to start?"
"Now. I don't have much going on, plus I just moved here. So the sooner, the better," I answered.

"Ah, that's nice. Welcome to Sterlington. It will be our greatest pleasure to have you. Please follow me to the back and we'll get you started," she said, leading me toward the back rooms.

We entered a decent-looking locker room. She showed me an empty locker and handed me a lock and key.

"Here you go," Bette said, holding out a packaged shirt and apron.

"Thank you," I said, smiling as I took them.

"You're welcome, dearie. Once you've settled yourself, join me at the front, okay?"

I nodded. She smiled and left. I pulled off my cardigan and t-shirt, slipped on the new uniform, tied the apron around me, and locked my things away. With the key tucked into my back pocket, I joined Bette at the front.

"Alright," she began, "the first thing we do is this: when people come in, we note how many and input them into the system. Their server

takes their order and brings it to us, we put it into the computer, and it goes to the
kitchen. Afterwards, when they're done, they come here to pay—you just press this button. Easy?"

"Yes, it's not complicated. I had some experience with this in high school," I replied, making her smile.
It was true. While living with the Tres Crescent Moon Pack, I had been required to attend school and get my education like everyone else. People didn't really like me, but I kept to myself and got through the years with only one thought in mind: getting out of that town.

"That's good. Okay, I'll leave you to it for an hour and come back to check on you. Sound good?"

"Yes."
With that, she left to handle her own tasks.
The bell rang, new customers came in, and I entered their numbers into the system. Servers brought me orders, I typed them in, and the kitchen got them instantly. That's how I spent the rest of the evening—taking orders, processing bills, tracking customers. Not once did I think about the events that took place in my pack.

Bette was impressed and decided to hire me full-time. I thanked her, then picked up a few groceries at the convenience store on my way back to the motel. After heating up pasta and eating in front of the TV, I showered and went to bed. My shift started at 8 a.m. tomorrow.

It had been a good day. A rough start, sure—but a good day nonetheless. I could get used to living here. With that thought, I fell asleep smiling.

Over the next couple of days, I worked and saved money for an apartment. The people here were kind and cheerful every day.

As the days passed, the bond I once had dissolved away. I no longer had a mind-link to the pack. Even though I was human, I'd had some connection through my mate's bond. I wondered if they'd realized I was gone, though I'd always lived in the shadows anyways

At *Joe & Mina's Diner*, I soon met the owners—an adorable couple who had been married for forty years. It was an arranged marriage, but they fell in love and were destined for each other.

As usual, I put my things away, grabbed my apron, and headed to the front for my hostess shift.

The diner might have been small, but it was always busy. Everyone loved the food, and the atmosphere was warm and welcoming—like family. Something I'd never really had. The Alpha and Luna had kept me hidden, so love and nurture were unknown to me.

The hours flew by. I stayed busy but enjoyed myself. While inputting an order for table six, Bette rushed out of the office toward me.

"Emery, are you available for an overtime shift on Friday?" she asked, sounding worried.

"Yes, of course. I don't have anything planned," I answered truthfully. I had no friends here yet. Back in the pack, I'd been avoided—an orphan, abandoned, and human, with nothing but mortality.

But here, people made me feel wanted and loved in their own way. I had never been happier.

That's because no one knows your true state.

"Oh, good, good. I'll need you and a couple of others," she said, pulling me out of my thoughts. I smiled.

"Sounds good," I replied. "What's happening on Friday?"

"We're having very important guests. Everything needs to be perfect."

"Okay, that makes sense. Don't worry—I'll come early and help decorate and clean," I offered.

"Great! Thank you," she said.

I smiled and got back to work, though curiosity lingered. Who were these guests that had Bette so nervous? I shrugged it off and finished my shift.
Today was just eight hours. Tomorrow was Thursday, my day off—a chance to go apartment hunting. Motel living couldn't last forever.

After work, I stopped by the convenience store for snacks and groceries, chatting with the owner, Mrs. Choi—a kind woman who had immigrated from Seoul when she was fifteen. Now she was happily married to her high school sweetheart.

"Hello, Mrs. Choi. How are you?"

"Ah, Emery, I'm good. How about you?"

"Very good, thanks," I said, gathering my usual items.

"How was work, dear?" she asked while scanning them.

"It was good. Tiring, but good. We're having some important guests on Friday—so that's exciting."

"Oh, very nice. Do you know who?"

"No idea. We'll see on Friday," I replied, handing her the cash.

"Have a good night, Mrs. Choi. See you tomorrow."

"You too," she said with a wave.

Back at the motel, I showered and fixed a microwave dinner. My nights were simple—eating, watching whatever was on TV, and waiting for sleep.

Tonight, I flipped to the news, but then decided to jailbreak the channels, hacking them until I picked up the ones from my pack. When it finally worked, the headline froze me in place.

"Chase Vance, son of Marcus and Rhoda Vance, was found dead in their home on November 4th at 8 a.m., alongside his girlfriend. They were discovered by the housekeeper.

Sources tell us no evidence has been found at this moment, and there are currently no suspects. The family requests any information that could help—and asks for privacy. Thank you, ladies and gentlemen. Good night."
I snapped out of it. It had been a few days since the murder, and still no evidence. Of course not. My tracks were covered well.

I chuckled, cleaned up my things, and went to bed. Sleep consumed me instantly.

CHAPTER 3:

Emery

Almost half a week has gone by since I arrived in this town. The first thing I did was get ready and gather whatever documents I had hidden in my room at the pack house. It's interesting how handy they come in when you need something. Once I locked the room door, I made my way down and took the first right to where I saw a few tall buildings. My morning looked quite busy, as finding a house is not easy. I entered the building and saw the office. I knocked on the door, they said to come in, and that's how I found myself sitting here in this tiny four-walled office, with broken air conditioning, writing down my information on the application. Once done, I looked it over before handing it to the staff member.

"Expect our call in 2 to 3 business days. It was very nice meeting you," the supervisor said. Getting up, I shook his hand. "We are open Monday through Friday. For any emergencies, here is the contact number for the superintendent on site for weekdays and weekends," he added as he handed me the business cards.

"Thank you. It was nice meeting you too," I said. Bidding my goodbye, I left.

I decided I would go and get a start on my laundry, so I made my way back to the motel. As I was walking towards the town plaza, suddenly, black cars drove in beside me, almost hitting the curb I was on.

"Fucking hell! Watch where you're going!" I yelled after the car. People passing by gave me weird looks. I didn't care.

The cars had these flags that looked quite familiar to me, but I couldn't pinpoint exactly where I'd seen them before. Hmm, where have I seen them, and why are they here? There were two small black cars in front, one large

limousine in the middle, followed by another two cars behind—same ones like the ones in the front.

Royalty, most likely...

I've seen these types of cars for royalty in movies. Maybe those are the guests for tomorrow. I stood there thinking, then pulled myself out of the trance and walked back to the motel.

Once in my room, away from everyone, I grabbed my laundry and headed out to the coin laundry place. Might as well do my laundry while I had the day off.

I changed into my lounge set outfit, packed my book, and turned my music on with the small swap-shop MP3 player I had purchased and loaded with songs I downloaded at the library. When in a new place, explore, familiarize yourself with everything you possibly can
Some time later

I loaded two washing machines and took a seat. I'd be here for a while. I had brought a book with me from the library and began reading.

About an hour in, I took a break to load my clothes into the dryer. I put the coins in and pressed start. Both would be done in an hour.

Might as well take a walk. I set the timer on my watch and headed out. I didn't have a proper fancy phone like most people here, but I did have a regular one.

I found myself in front of the diner. Of course, it's everyone's favorite place to go. It wasn't lunch yet, still brunch, so I figured I might as well grab something to eat. I walked in, and one of the employees I work with—her name is Penny—saw me and smiled.

"Emery, hey girl, what are you doing here on your day off?" she asked. "Nothing much. Filed a few apartment applications, and now I'm currently doing my laundry, so I came here to grab something to eat."

"Of course, you're in the right place. Let me show you to your table," she said. I followed her lead.

I sat down and she handed me the menu. "Drinks?" she asked.

"Um, an iced tea. Thanks."

"No problem, coming right up," she said, walking off happily. See, this is why I love working here. The environment is never negative, always positive. I don't know why I even feel happy—especially after I killed someone in cold blood...

My blood ran cold at that thought. The news hasn't reported anything new. I worry, of course. I am responsible for the future Alpha's life, and I took him away from the world. I'm not going to say he deserved it, but he did. Soulmates are destined for each other. I just wish he wasn't destined for me. Everything would've been easier if he had rejected me. I would've gladly accepted it.

A cup was placed in front of me, pulling me out of my trance. I've been doing that a lot, I've noticed. What can you do? Anxiety does this.

"So, have you decided on what you'd like?" Penny asked. Shoot—I zoned out and forgot to check the menu.

"Um, can I get the crispy chicken sandwich, with lettuce, tomato, and mayo?" I asked after a quick scan of the menu.

"Sure," she said and went to input it into the computer. She came back and took a seat across from me.

"I've noticed you've been zoning out. Everything okay?" she asked, genuinely concerned.

"Yeah, I'm fine. I guess I'm just still getting used to the new atmosphere around me," I replied.

"Oh, I get that. Trust me, girl, I was in your shoes a few years back," she told me, and I listened to her story.

After her story, we were both chatting and eating. It was her break, so she joined me.

"Did you see the black cars?" she asked suddenly.

"Yes, yes I did. Do you know who they are?" I asked, hoping she did.

"Not a clue. But I'm pretty sure it's the important guests for tomorrow. I've seen the cars a couple of times but never really remembered who it was."

"Ah, okay. Makes sense. Are you working tomorrow?" I asked.
"No, my cousin's daughter is getting baptized tomorrow, so good luck to you." She laughed. I glared at her and soon enough, I laughed too.

My timer had gone off a long time ago, so I paid and tipped for my meal, then headed back to the laundry. I grabbed my things and went to my room. I didn't want to waste any more time there, so I folded my clothes inside.

As I was folding, my phone rang. I answered.

"Hello, is this Emery?" the person asked.

"Yes, this is her."

"We met earlier today. I'm calling to inform you that you've been approved for the apartment on the 5th floor."

"Oh wow, that was quick. Thank you very much, I really appreciate it," I told them.

"You're very welcome. You may move in whenever you'd like. Come by for the set of keys."

"For sure. See you."

"See you too. Welcome to the building."

I thanked them and hung up. I squealed with joy and continued folding my laundry. I packed it away in the bag, along with my other stuff. This weekend, I would move in. For now, I should at least order a mattress, since I won't have any furniture yet. I found a furniture store in the phone book and placed an order for a mattress. It would be delivered the following Sunday. So, Sunday morning I should have the keys and be ready to move in.

Filled with joy, I took a shower and headed to bed so I could go in earlier than expected to help set up. I fell asleep shortly afterwards.

CHAPTER 4:

Dexter

We drove into Sterlington, the same old town for the past ten years now. Nothing different, always the same. I sat in the back seat of the limo while my men sat in front.

As we rounded the corner, a sweet scent of peppermint and lavender filled my nostrils. I rolled down the window, trying to find out whose scent it belonged to. No luck—too many people. I sat back.

Some random person yelled, "Fucking hell, watch where you're going!" My men looked at me, silently asking if we should stop. I shook my head no.
"My liege, we have arrived at your home for the week," my driver said after some time.

I nodded as he parked the car. One of my men opened the door while another led me inside. I love visiting small towns—always some business happening, or sometimes just simple pleasure. I wonder which one it will be this visit.

Once inside, I took a seat at the head of the table. "What is the plan?" The head of security, Jeff, answered, "You have lunch scheduled at Joe and Mina's Diner, sir."

"Okay. Anything else?" I asked.

"Just casual business meetings with certain shops," Jeff replied.
I nodded and dismissed them.

I walked around the room, stopping at the window in the study. The double doors opened to a balcony. I stepped out, basking in the view of the town. I saw how everyone stopped and looked at the cars and our entrance. It's always the same whenever I visit a new place.

A girl caught my eye in the distance. Hard to miss—she was wearing a bright green outfit. Her hair was tied in a ponytail as she walked around, then stopped at the diner.

Hmm. I wonder if she's new, or if I've just never seen her before. Likely both. I'm always observant in any setting.

My name is Dexter, the Alpha Prince of the Midnight Royal Crescent Moon Pack. Our pack has the strongest werewolves anyone has ever seen. Ever since I turned twenty-one, my father has entrusted me with the family business—going on business trips, making changes when needed, gathering opinions, and more.

Being Royal is not easy. People think it is, but it isn't. Being a Royal Alpha is even harder—the roles and responsibilities are more than most could handle. That's why my father made sure I was trained, that I knew everything like the back of my hand, before he stepped down.

My family is always my number one priority, and it is my duty to protect everyone in my pack. I do not have a mate yet, though I hope that someday I will, whenever the Moon Goddess decides.

I scratched my beard, shook the thoughts away, and headed back inside to take care of pending documents and the calendar for my time here.

By the time I finished, it was late. Dinner had been brought to me earlier but sat untouched. I put the documents into a folder and locked them away in the drawer. Calling it a night, I got ready for bed.

Sleep consumed me quickly. Werewolves are not affected by jet lag like humans are. We coexist with humans, though only some know of us while others do not. I prefer to keep it that way. Safety comes first, and I will not let anyone jeopardize that.

CHAPTER 5:

Emery

The next morning, I woke up earlier than usual, practically with the sun rising. I got dressed after my quick morning shower routine. For such occasions, we were required to wear black pants, white button-up shirts, and our aprons along with our name tags.

I brushed and French-braided my hair, using a bit of hairspray to keep the strands in place. After spraying some perfume, I grabbed my things and headed out.

I reached the back of the diner where the employee entrance was. Knocking twice, the main cook opened it.

"Morning," I said.

"Morning," he grumbled, stepping aside to let me in.

I nodded and walked past him, heading straight to the locker room. After shoving my stuff inside, I went to the floor, where I was met with Bette and the other employees.

"Good morning, ladies and gentlemen," she began. "I apologize for asking you all to come in extra early, but as some of you know, this occasion happens yearly. It is required that everything be in place and perfect. We've satisfied our guests before, and we will continue to do so.

"As for our new member—she isn't familiar with our important guests, so let me explain. Emery, since you are very new to our team,

each year on this day we host very important guests: the Midnight Royal Family. That's why everyone is on edge and why everything must be perfect. Hopefully, this won't stress you out. Now, everyone be on your best behavior and have a great morning. Let's get started." She clapped her hands and dismissed us.
Midnight Royal? Why does that sound familiar?

I got to work at my station. Another employee explained to me that during the morning and lunch, the diner would be closed for our guests. Everyone in town knew this. No wonder some were on edge. It's not every day royalty comes here, so I understood the weight of the assignment.

I set up the computer, making sure everything was running properly. Each person working today had their role and duty. Double-checking wouldn't hurt, so I gave it a triple check. I loaded the paper into both registers, rebooted the second register, and made sure everything was in order. Now, all we had to do was wait…

"They will be arriving shortly," Bette announced. And almost on cue, they pulled up—the cars and the limo.

I straightened up, shoulders back, chin high, and waited. I saw the driver rushing to open the limo door. A tall man stepped out, though I couldn't make out who it was…

The diner door opened. Bette greeted them as we all bowed. The man entered, followed by his security team.

Bette led him toward me. The protocol was simple, but as soon as the man came closer and I got a good look at him, all I could think was—
SHIT!!

CHAPTER 6:

Emery
SHIT!!!!
I am so dead… The Midnight Royal is actually the Midnight Royal Crescent Moon Pack… oh damnnnnnn!!!!

I snapped out of it as fast as possible.
"This is our new member, Emery, Your Highness. Emery, say hello and please take down his information," Bette tells me. I smile and nod.

"Hello, I'm Emery. Welcome to our diner. I will be your hostess for the morning. May I have your name and the number of guests that will be joining you, Your Highness?" I asked, almost out of breath, trying to keep calm.

He chuckles. "It's a pleasure to meet you. My name is Prince Dex, and there will be about ten joining me."

I nod as I input his information.

"Your Majesty and gentlemen, if you would oblige and follow me to your table," I say with a big smile. Prince Dex smiles and steps aside as if to say, *you may pass.*

I walk ahead of them, keeping my composure and calm. I lead them to their table, which has a deep blue tablecloth with matte black silverware and plates. Stepping aside, I let His Majesty sit down first. Once they've all settled in their seats, I hand them each a menu.

"What could I get you started with?" I ask, pen and notepad ready.

"A bottle of your best wine for me and my guests," he says. I nod as I write it down.

"Coming right up." I bow and leave.

Dexter

My team and I arrived at the diner. Once I entered, the scent I'd smelled yesterday was here. The manager of the diner, my parents' old friend, greeted me.

The girl I'd seen yesterday in bright clothing was our hostess. She left after getting our drink order. We didn't require the menu, as the chef already knew all of our orders.

She came back quickly, opening the bottle in front of us. I was impressed. She poured me a glass first, then my guests.

"Thank you," I said.

"You're very welcome, Your Majesty," she replied. "Anything else, or would you like some more time?"

"The chef already knows what I'll be having, and what my guests will be having as well. Thank you." I nodded slightly.

She nods and excuses herself.
"Before you go," I stop her. She turns back, facing me. "What is your name?"

"It's Emery," she says, looking at me as if she has not been introduced to me, without realizing that she didn't address me properly, just gave me a straightforward answer. I must say, it definitely intrigues me to find out more about her.

"I mean, what is Emery short for?" I ask again.

"Emerald, Your Highness," she answers. I can sense some hesitation in her tone, as if she didn't want to reveal her full name.

"Magnificent name," I said. She gave me a small smile. I smiled back, and she excused herself.

Emerald… magnificent name indeed. This will be interesting—peeling her layers slowly but surely. Something about her has my pulse racing and my wolf stirring out of control. A human is making me feel something I have never felt before.

Emery

Really?? Oh no. What if he finds out…? No, he won't. Just remain calm. They can sense a change in pulse, sense fear, anxiety, etc. This is not the time to lose your shit. You have a job to do and to make Bette proud during their visit here. From what I found out, the royal family makes this trip every two years as tradition, and ever since they've expanded their business, I have a feeling their visits may become more frequent.

I refocused my attention on the tasks at hand. And yes, I know very well who the prince is. Oh yes—at all the formal events I've been to with the Alpha and Luna, everyone knows who he is and who the

Midnight Crescent Moon Pack is. They're the strongest werewolves anyone has ever known. No one dares to disobey or disrespect them.

I am worried, because what if he recognizes me and who I am? Our head chef will be serving their meals shortly, and I shall remain at my post until His Majesty requires my attention. And when he does, I must not reveal any more information. However, my gut tells me that will be an impossible task.

Throughout the day I took other orders for pick-up, since dining in wasn't open while royalty was here.

As a customer left, I noticed Prince Dex waving to me. *Here goes nothing,* I thought as I approached their table.

"Yes, Your Highness?" I asked politely.

"We're done with our plates," he says.

I nodded and began clearing them away. When I was done, I went back to them and asked if they would like dessert. Some said yes, and some said no, since they were full.

The chef and his team brought out a cart full of different dessert dishes for them to choose from. I stood back, unless I was needed. My nerves had calmed down, which was good.

Bette tapped me on the shoulder. I turned to look at her.

"Everything good?"

"Everything is going according to plan," I responded, making her smile.

She nodded and headed off to her office.

A few more hours passed before His Highness and his guests decided to leave.

I checked them out and bid them goodbye. Prince Dex stayed a bit behind.

"Your Highness, is everything alright?" I asked.

He came close to me. My heart began racing as he leaned forward and whispered,

"I feel like I've sensed you from somewhere… but where?"

I chuckled nervously before replying, "Uh, I don't think that would have been possible, as today was the first time I met you, Your Highness." I lied straight through my teeth.

Dexter

I bid my goodbye to the hostess as I left her standing there. Her heart was beating fast, as if she were nervous. Well, I have that charm when it comes to women.

Her scent was definitely familiar to me. But what I can't pinpoint is where I sensed it before. It must not have been here. My mind goes back to what Bette said—that she was new to town. Hmm. I'll need more information on her.

We were all seated in the car as the driver took us back to our house for the time being during our stay here.

"How was the food, Your Highness?" Jeff asked me.

"It was good, as always," I replied.

"Good, we're glad."

"Hope you enjoyed it as well," I said, and they all agreed.
We arrived shortly after, and each went to their own studies—most likely to rest after a good meal. I did too. After answering a few calls, I laid down for a few hours.

But my thoughts wandered back to Emerald. With the decision made, I will make it my mission to get to know her. And I know exactly where to start.
I smirked.

CHAPTER 7:

Emery

After the guests had left, we opened for dinner service. People came in once they saw we were open. Dinner service was a rush and a thrill all at once.

A few hours later, my coworkers and I stayed extra to help the kitchen staff clean up. When we were done, Bette surprised us with pizza and drinks to celebrate a successful day. It's a tradition that has been followed for many years now.

Eventually, I made it home, took a shower, and went straight to sleep. *Dream flashback*

I was in a ballroom hall. People were frozen in fear until one of them said, *"The Alpha Killer is here in this room at this exact moment."*

They gasped, and I smiled as I looked at everyone's panicked state. I chuckled darkly as I stepped out of my hiding spot…

"Emery?" a voice asked.

"Me!" I smiled.

I jolted out of sleep and saw the clock read 3 a.m.

Great, just great. I plopped back down on my bed, unable to get the dream out of my head. *Who was that? How did they find out? Did they?* All of these questions ran through my mind. I groaned, completely losing my sleep.

I stood up from bed and went to the living room, sitting on the window bay sill and looking out into the town's lights. I hadn't had a nightmare this bad since I was a young girl.

Before I knew it, the sun was rising. Might as well get ready for nothing—I wasn't working today. I wasn't going to try to see whether or not the dream would continue.

I took off my clothes and hopped into my very warm shower, the water hitting my muscles and instantly relaxing them. I washed my body and hair, and when I was done, I wrapped a towel around me. Just as I stepped out of the bathroom, my phone rang. Assuming it was Bette, I picked up.

"Hello?"

"Hello Emerald, how are you?" the voice asked. Something about it reminded me of the voice in my dream, but I shook off the thought and replied,

"Good, thank you. Um, may I ask who you are?"

They chuckled. "Oh, how silly of me. It's me, Prince Dexter. I asked Bette for your number. I hope you don't mind," Dex replied.
"Oh, Your Highness, no, I don't mind," I said, feeling some relief but also anxiety.

"You may call me Dex." That's all he said, so I agreed, and we got into a conversation.

Two hours later, the phone call had led me into my closet, looking for a dress for lunch with His Majesty. I found a semi-long floral maxi dress with a braided belt and a denim jacket, paired with some flats. I had purchased a couple of dresses for the upcoming warm season.

After blow-drying my hair, I braided it, grabbed my cross-body bag, and headed out, locking my door behind me. I made sure no one saw me.

Downstairs, sure enough, there he was—looking very dashing indeed.

He had two men with him, completely understandable. I approached him, slightly bowing my head.

"Hello Emerald, you look lovely, and thank you for agreeing to join me for lunch."

"Hi. Thank you for the compliment and the invitation. You look dashing, Your Majesty."

He smiled at my compliment and nodded. He stepped aside, opened the car door, and gestured for me to get in first. I felt his hand on my back—electricity shot through my veins, and I had a vision…

"After you," he said.

"Oh, thank you." I slid into the car and buckled myself. He followed after, gave a sign to his driver, and we drove off. My mind was not here, but elsewhere…

As we drove to the restaurant, we made small chatter. He asked me what I liked.

"I like to read, go for walks, simple things," I told him.

He nodded. I asked him the same.

"I've always enjoyed reading, playing chess, riding horses… typical things."

"Oh, that's nice," I responded, picturing him on a horse before refocusing on the conversation.

"How about you? What do you like to do?" he asked.

"Not a lot. I'm an introvert and tend to stick to myself—very quiet. Reading is one of my favorite things to do," I replied, not sharing too much.

The car pulled up, cutting our conversation short. The doors opened, and we stepped out and went inside the restaurant.

We were seated immediately. Soon after we sat down, the waitress started batting her eyelashes at the Prince. I rolled my eyes, clearly seeing how hard she was trying to gain his attention. When she realized it wasn't working, she took our drink orders. I ordered an iced tea, and so did he.

She nodded and walked away. While we looked at the menu—fancy dishes that didn't surprise me, though I said nothing—he asked,

"Anything you would like to try?"

"Uh, not really. I think I'll just go with the pasta," I said. He nodded.

The waitress returned. I ordered chicken Alfredo pasta, and he ordered steak with mashed potatoes and vegetables on the side. She nodded and left"Tell me, where else have you traveled?" I asked, starting the conversation again.

Eventually, our lunch ended, and we left shortly after. He took me to the beach next.

We stayed there for hours, talking, laughing, dipping our feet in the water. The sun began to set, and I sighed, taking in the sight.

"Shall we head to my place?" I asked, turning toward him.

He smiled, stood up, and extended his hand toward me. I placed mine in his, and he helped me up. We walked to the car, got in, and he told the driver my address.

We arrived at my place shortly. He told his driver to go for a bit, and the car drove off. Keys in hand, we entered the building and headed straight to my apartment.

Before unlocking my door, I turned to him.

"Uh, my place is nothing fancy. Just an FYI."

He chuckled. "Do not worry, I will not judge."

I nodded and opened the door. We both entered. As soon as the door closed, his mouth was on mine—fighting for dominance, needing control. I fought back with the same energy and need.

Hands were everywhere. He had me pinned against the wall, my hands above my head as he kissed me roughly. His kisses came strong, making my whole body burn with raging desire.

We moved to the bedroom, clothes ripped off on the way. I stood in my matching set, while he was down to his Calvin Klein boxers— fully erect bulge straining against the fabric.

"Are you sure?" his raspy voice asked as he laid me down on the bed.

"Yes," I whispered, breathless.

That's all it took for him to lunge at me—kissing and sucking on my skin, leaving hickeys, drawing moans from my mouth.

The last pieces of clothing came off us. With one stroke, he thrust inside me. I hissed.

"Shit, sorry," he said, slowing down, pulling out gently, and pushing back in slowly—eliciting soft moans.

I was indeed a virgin… but not anymore, especially after tonight. The pain turned into pleasure, my hands gripping and scratching his back as the night filled with excitement and ecstasy.

He finally came and collapsed next to me, pulling me into his arms. He reached below us, pulled the blanket over, and planted a kiss on my forehead.

I fell into a deep slumber.

Emery

The next morning, I woke up sore, a reminder of last night. I looked to my side, seeing him still asleep. I got up from the bed and headed straight into the bathroom, turning the shower on. I hopped in, letting the hot water run down my back. Leaning forward against the wall, I stood there thinking about what happened…

All I knew was that it shouldn't happen again. My thoughts were cut off when his arms wrapped around my waist and pulled me into his chest, soft kisses being planted against my neck. A soft moan escaped my mouth as his hand snaked down to my perfectly smooth mound. I turned around and he kissed me, wasting no time between us.

"Good morning," his husky voice melted me.

"Morning," I replied.

After our very steamy shower, we dried off. I put on sweats and a shirt, while he wore the same clothes as yesterday.

His phone rang. Excusing himself, he stepped away while I went to the kitchen.

Dexter

"Morning, your highness. Sorry to intrude this early in the morning," Jeff spoke.

"Morning, not a problem at all. How can I help?" I replied.

"Alright, we have some news. But it would be best to discuss it in person, sir."

"Understandable. Send the car to this address." I sent it through text.

"Yes, your highness," Jeff responded. With that being said, I ended the call.

"Coffee?" I heard from behind me. I turned around with a smile and said, "Gladly."

CHAPTER 8

Emery

I'd be lying if I said I didn't eavesdrop… but hey, it's not like he was trying to be quiet. I couldn't fully hear what the other side of the phone said, but what I could understand was that there was some sort of news.

"I'll be leaving soon, but no worries, we shall meet again," Dex spoke after some time. I nodded and sipped on my coffee.

Soon enough, his men came to pick him up. I walked him to the door. As he stepped out, he suddenly changed his mind and pulled me in for a kiss. We kissed goodbye. I waved, closed the door, and locked it.

I walked to my balcony. Stepping out, I looked down at the car. As if he sensed me, he looked up, waved, and got in. I sighed once the car was far enough.

I decided to clean up the house a bit; not much else for me to do. I have to wait until he returns or calls. I *could* call him too, but I'd rather not disturb him since he has to deal with the murder that I am behind.

Each time I try to act normal, I can't. I know what I did. Do I regret it? Maybe a little. This is not the life I imagined myself having, but who knows—maybe it's all part of the Goddess's plan.

Let's just hope her plan doesn't end with my identity being revealed, because I really do love this little town and the life I've built so far. I really hope I get to live a long life.

Dexter

We reached the house. As I walked inside, I saw my men gathered, waiting for me to sit down before we began.

"I hear you have something to discuss with me. Let's hear it?"
Jeff nodded, then began.

"There has been a murder—the soon-to-be Alpha of the Trés Moon Crescent Pack, to be specific. It is said there are no suspects, which is why this has piqued a lot of interest. They're asking for an audience with you, my lord."
I sat there listening as he continued. "They're hoping you'll accept their invitation."

After some deep thinking, they sat in anticipation, waiting for my response. I agreed.

"When do they want an audience with me?" I asked.

"As soon as possible. The Alpha requests it," Jeff said. I nodded.

"We shall leave at once," I said. The meeting adjourned, they nodded, and began to prepare.

I called Emery. She picked up.

"Hey, gorgeous," I said.

She chuckled. "Hey, handsome. To what do I owe the pleasure of this phone call?"

"I wanted to hear your voice and share some news with you, if that's okay."

"Yes, that is completely fine with me," she said.

I told her how amazing our night was, and that I must go away for a business matter. But not to worry, because I'd be back soon. She was very understanding. We talked a bit more until Jeff said it was time to go. Emery and I bid our goodbyes. I followed my men out to the car, and once we were all settled, the drive began.

After the discussion with the family, my men and I went to my hometown first before we headed off to the Trés Moon Crescent Pack.

"Gather all the information on the lost mate and report immediately." Upon my orders, they scurried away. I took this chance to give Emery a call. Can you tell I'm becoming obsessed with hearing her voice?

On the second ring, she answered. My girl is eager to hear my voice, it seems.

"Well, well, to what extent do I owe this pleasure to you, Your Royal Highness?" she teased.

"Good afternoon, milady," I replied. She chuckled.

"I'm sorry it took me so long to call. Business has been chaotic. How are you?"

"I understand. I'm good. How are you?" she replied.

We made small chatter.

"I miss you," I told her honestly. It was true. In such a short time, I'd gotten close to her—and I'm not usually an open person.

"I miss you too," she said.

I smiled at her confession, and it made me feel good that she missed me as much as I missed her.

I asked what she was doing, and we kept the chatter going as much as we could—until my men burst into the office.

"My liege, we found information regarding the lost mate!" One of them noticed I was on a call and quickly apologized.

"Emery, I'll have to call you back later. You understand?" I told her. She said yes, and we bid our goodbyes. I turned to my men and demanded everything.

CHAPTER 9

Emery

"Lost mate"… That's all I heard before we bid our goodbyes.

I started pacing back and forth. This is not looking good. I slowed my breathing as much as I could. This is not good… They're close—but not close enough. Yet it feels like the walls are closing in on me, with nowhere to escape, nowhere to hide.

I stopped and pulled myself together before I got any weird looks from people.

Taking another deep breath, I walked inside the diner, ready for my shift.
Bette noticed I wasn't myself. I told her I just missed home, that was all. She understood and gave me a hug.

No one can find me. No one *must* find me. I've already accepted the fate of my consequences when I killed them both…

I shook it off and threw myself into work. By the time I finished, I was exhausted from the long shift. I stripped down, pulled on a shirt, and climbed into bed, falling asleep as soon as my head touched the pillow. It's been a few days since I last heard from Dex. I understood— business and all. I shook the feelings away, grabbed my food, and walked over to the sofa. I sat down with the TV on. I took the first bite of my spaghetti when the news came on (werewolf channel news). I may or may not have found a way to get the information the regular news wouldn't show.

"This just in... Royalty has flown down to meet with the Trés Moon Pack regarding the murder of two members: the future Alpha and his significant other..."

I choked, took a breath, and kept eating.
"Your Highness, do you have any comments?"
"I have but one comment: whoever the suspect is, we will get to the bottom of it and make sure to lay out the proper consequences. That is all. Thank you."

Reporters tried to get more out of him. I burst out laughing at how pathetic they could be. The killer—me—is free and in hiding, and I made sure not to leave any evidence behind.

But it *is* funny how I fooled the Royal Prince. Him, being powerful and all... Don't get me wrong, he is great in bed, but not so smart. I sighed, sat back, changed the channel to a chick-flick movie, and finished the rest of my dinner.

Dexter

The swarm of reporters was nothing new to me. As I got in the car, my bodyguards fended them off. We settled inside and drove off to the pack house of Trés Moon.

We'd been here multiple times. This time it was different, considering their son was killed in cold blood alongside his girlfriend. I guessed he didn't have a mate yet.

We arrived shortly after, greeted by Alpha Eric and Luna Martha. We bowed and shook hands.

"Welcome, Your Highness."

"Thank you. Apologies for the circumstances that brought us here today," I replied. The Luna nodded alongside her husband.

"Shall we take this inside? Too many ears outside," Alpha Eric said, stepping aside.

"Yes, that is most wise," I responded.

Following them inside, we settled in the Alpha's office, more private for our discussion.

"I noticed that your son's girlfriend was beside him when they were found, correct? Did he not have a mate, considering he was over 18?" I began the questioning.

The Alpha and Luna exchanged a look of uncertainty.

"In order to help you find the murderer and put them away, any small details help," I said.

Luna Martha sighed. "Yes, our son did have a mate."

Had? "And where is his mate?"

"They disappeared… maybe got kidnapped. Our son's relationship with her was not the best. He didn't like her but accepted her because of my wife. She wanted a girl, but unfortunately, we were not blessed with a daughter, only a son," the Alpha explained.

"Could she be the one behind this?" I asked.

"We don't believe so. She kept herself in darkness, in the shadows. Not very social. I don't think she could do this," Luna answered.

I nodded, thinking deeply. Jealousy… lack of confidence… hiding in the shadows. All motives for murder.

"If she has been kidnapped, have there been any ransom notes or contact? Considering that's what usually happens in cases like this."
"No, Your Highness. No such attempts have been made," the Alpha answered.

"Well, it seems we have one answer. She wasn't kidnapped. She most likely disappeared on her own. As you said, she wasn't a social person, so it's safe to say she left—especially with the current events."

After a brief discussion, I asked one more question.
"What is the lost mate's name? Any details of her description can help with this case."

"Her name is Emery. We don't know her full name—it was never revealed to us. She's about 5'6 with medium-length hair…"

The description sounded familiar, and I could only think of one person with that name and matching description.

I doubted she was behind the murders—she seemed too innocent. Coincidence? Maybe…

"I'll have my men look into all the details and the friends your son hung out with. We won't pin this on only one suspect at the moment. Please provide us with their contact information. Sounds good?"

They nodded.

"Alright then, keep us posted and I will do the same. We *will* catch the killer, and you will get the closure you deserve." I put a hand on their shoulders.

"Thank you, Your Highness."

I nodded and bid my goodbyes.

"Where to?" Jeff asked.

"Home, please."

The car drove off with my instruction

CHAPTER 10:

Emery

I was dragged into a ballroom, everyone seated, lights blinding like the sun itself when the fold was removed.

"You!" someone screamed out.

I looked at them, not recognizing them at first... then it clicked. Him...
My phone's constant ringing jolted me awake. I answered it, grumpy. "Good morning, sorry to have woken you up at this hour. Calling to tell you I'll be coming back in a week or two," Dex said.

I told him that was alright. We talked for a bit and ended the call. I went back to sleep.

When I woke again, I took a shower and got dressed. Since I was off today, I decided to go grocery shopping and maybe grab some new things at the shopping center plaza. Once my grocery trip was done, I unpacked everything and went back to the plaza for clothes and other items. By the time I finished, it was already dark outside. That was fine, I came prepared with pepper spray and... my gun. The same one I had used. I promised myself I wouldn't use it again unless absolutely necessary.

I sighed in relief when I entered my building. Checking my mail, I found an invitation to the *Annual Werewolf Ball*. Hmm. Interesting. But how did I get it? Maybe I'll attend... but would it be risky? I thought as I turned to toss it into the garbage, only to be met with complete darkness…

Meanwhile, at Prince Dexter's suite, gathered around with his men.

"What information have we gathered on Emery?" Dexter asked.

"Well, sir, we know she was abandoned by her family, left in the care of the Tres Moon Crescent family at the age of 10. By age 18, their son and she were fated to be mates," his right-hand man answered.

"Do we have anything on how she was treated during her time there?" Dexter pressed, hoping for more intel.

His right-hand man continued, "I believe, from what Luna mentioned, that Emery mostly kept to herself, in the shadows. Never engaging much."

"Alright, if that is all, we should bring her in for questioning. Get everything ready," he ordered. The men nodded and scurried out.

I woke up in a chair. Great. Just great. Well, if this isn't karma of some sort, then I don't know what to expect.

Rule number one: never turn your back to enemies, or anyone. Lesson learned.

Looking around, I realized no one was guarding me. I tried to budge my hands out of their binds, but no luck. My chair squeaked slightly, alerting someone outside. A figure entered.

"Well, looks like someone is awake," the mysterious person said.

"Ya think?" I shot back, sarcastically. "Who are you?"

"Uh huh. My identity is not your concern. What *is* your concern is the ball."

"The ball?" I asked.

"Yes, the ball. You must attend it. If you don't, you'll miss out on the fun… Miss Emery. Or shall I say, Emerald?" he laughed, stepping closer.

"How do you know my name?" I demanded.

"I've been watching you here and there. Which brings me to my next point… the Prince. His men are currently looking for the killer."

I smirked. "I *am* the killer. Yet they're daft and haven't found me."

"That, my dear, is where you're wrong. They may think they know who you are, and while they haven't confirmed it yet, they are getting closer. Do not be fooled. As we speak, they've gathered enough information. Once they're able to fully pin the identity to the suspect… it won't look good for you. Which is why you must go to the ball. No matter what choice you make, the outcome won't look good. So, my dear killer… what do you choose?"

I sat there, thinking about his words. Either choice might end my life. I already knew and had been prepared for the day they found out. I just hadn't expected to fall in love with… him.

"I guess I'll make an appearance. What have I got to lose?" I replied.

He nodded, grinning, then untied me. As we walked out of the warehouse, I asked, "What will I get from this?"

"I'm not sure. But you were chosen by the Moon Goddess herself. Your life has a purpose. You must find it. Until then, I wish you luck. You'll definitely need it."

Before I could respond, I was met with darkness once again. When I woke next, I was in my bed. Groaning at the blasting sunlight through the curtains, I dragged myself up and washed my face with cold water. My mind replayed last night's events.

Maybe I should go to the ball. I'll definitely need a dress. Guess I have to go shopping again.

I groaned, got dressed, and since I didn't start work until later today, I headed to the town's mall plaza. Once there, I searched for a store that sold ball gowns, dresses, and shoes. Entering, the bell chimed, and a cheerful young saleswoman greeted me.

"Hi there, how can I help you today?" she asked brightly.

"Uh, I have a gala… a ball next week, and I need a dress. I have no idea where to start since it'll be my first one in a while," I admitted.

"You've come to the right place. Let's get started," she said, whisking me to a dressing room. Moments later, she returned with an armful of dresses in every color and style.

This is going to take some time, I thought with a sigh. Best to get started fast.

CHAPTER 11:

Dexter

"Sir, everything is coming into place with the preparation of the ball room. If there is anything you'd like us to add, please do let us know. Your satisfaction is our most important thing." I looked around the room, feeling good.

"No, that will be all. Thank you." I say. They nodded and bowed before departing.

"Any news." I ask my men.

"No, your highness." they replied

"Alright thank you, if anything does come up, let me know." I replied. My men nodded and we headed on out. I pulled my phone out, shooting a quick *I miss you* text to Emery.

She replied back with *I miss you too.* It put a smile on my face as we drove off. This year's gala/ball will be held in the same town as the annual dinner. I have attended such events since I was a young boy.

Emery

After 3 hours, yes 3 hours, I found the dress and shoes as well as the jewelry I'll be needing for the ball.

I rushed to the dinner with the stuff I bought as I did not have time to run home. Thankfully, my uniform is in my locker. I burst the diner's door and Bette got startled.

"My dear, are you alright?" she asked me.

"I am alright, I was running late as my little shopping thing took a little too long. Who knew women needed so many things for special events?" I responded with a chuckle. Bette laughed, "I have been wondering the same thing, go on, take a few minutes to yourself and come out when you are ready", she tells me and pats my shoulder. I thank her and head on to the back of the diner. It was a struggle to stuff my locker with shopping bags, but not the dress bag. I hung that up in her office as I did not want it to get crinkled and wrinkled.

A few minutes later I was good to join my gals on the floor. It was dinner time so lots of customers came in and out. We were busy, I loved every minute of it. Once my shift was over, I decided to call a cab home, as I had too many things to carry and I was quite exhausted. As soon as I reached home, I dropped everything by the door, I laid the dress onto the sofa and went to bed. Sleep consumed within minutes..

~One week later, the night of the Ball~

The day of the ball has finally arrived. It's not until 7pm, so I have a lot of time to go and get my hair done.

I made the appointment last night, for today. With the time of the appointment nearing, I got dressed into simple sweats and a crop top and headed on to the salon.
As soon as I sat in the chair, the hairstylist began. This will take a while, is all I thought to myself as I relaxed in the chair. There were many services, so while my hair was being worked on, the nail lady

was doing my manicure. It was quite nice and definitely relaxing as the whole week has been stressful with everything that has happened.

Work is amazing and I enjoy it a lot, so the little time I get for relaxation, I make sure to fully soak in it. As who knows what the events of my life will take place.

Dexter

"It is looking quite good, have we double checked everything to ensure it has no issues?" I asked, looking at the ballroom set up.

"Everything is going according to plan and schedule. All the lights, wiring, switches have been double checked, routers, doors, carpets and much more have been properly laid out plus inspected, your highness" one of the event coordinators told me.

"Good, good. If you'll excuse me" I say, he bows and I take my leave. I haven't spoken with Emery for a while, I wonder if she is okay. I did not mention to her I was back in town, sent her texts here and there, but that's about it. I got into my car and drove home to get ready.

Hmm, should I call Bette and ask about Emery.. ? I understand that the diner has been busy as it always is and usually from the tone of Emery during our calls, she sounds quite exhausted.

However, I can't help,but think that there may be more to her as she won't tell me much else. I do not pry when it comes to her, but should I have done so? Would that have gotten her to open up to me? So many questions, yet so many little answers..especially from the woman I have come to love. *LOVE..a small yet powerful word and feeling. Love makes people do crazy things.*

All I can do is get lost in my thoughts and prepare for tonight's event.

CHAPTER 12:

Emery

Hair, nails, and makeup all done, I hardly recognized myself as I pulled on my dress. A deep maroon-red mermaid gown with silky lace sleeves. Shoes to match, velvet maroon-red, and a sequined clutch for my small necessities. My hair was pinned up, soft curls framing my face. Smokey eyes, dark as the night, and lipstick red as blood.

A car horn outside grabbed my attention. One last look in the mirror, time to go. I slipped my keys and phone into my clutch, locked the door, and headed downstairs.

The driver stepped forward as I approached. "Good evening, ma'am. Do you require any assistance with your gown?"

Eh, what the heck. "Yes, I actually do, if you wouldn't mind," I replied, eliciting a small chuckle from him.
"Not at all," he said as he gently lifted the train of my gown and helped me into the limo.

Once on the road, I double-checked my clutch, making sure the invitation was still inside. Satisfied, I leaned back and let myself enjoy the drive.
Twenty minutes later, the car pulled up to the banquet hall. The driver came around again, offering his assistance as I stepped out. My gown spread behind me beautifully. I thanked him and made my way up the grand stairs, past the double doors, guards stationed on either side.

"Your invitation, Miss?" one of them asked.

I pulled it out of my clutch and handed it over. He nodded and gestured me toward the banquet hall. Smiling politely, I walked on.

Two more guards opened the doors. Guests filled the room, voices mingling with the sound of live jazz. Some eyes turned toward me, lingering for a moment before moving on. I ignored the stares and headed for the champagne table.

Dexter

Guests poured into the hall as I stood on the balcony, watching them laugh and socialize.

The double doors opened again. Someone entered. All eyes shifted to her… I couldn't help but wonder who she was.

"Your Highness," Jeff's voice cut into my thoughts, "we got an anonymous tip that the killer is here tonight, somewhere in this hall."

I nodded, my eyes narrowing. *Let the fun begin…*

I made my rounds, greeting the many guests who had RSVPed for this night, though none of them knew how truly *special* it would be.

While speaking with the Tres Crescent Moon Alpha and Luna, Jeff approached again.

"Sire, pardon the interruption. We've finally pinned the identity. However… you may not believe it. With respect, my advice is to give them a chance to come forward. But then again, I know you will do as you think best."

His words came so quickly I could only nod.

"If you'll excuse me," I said to the Alpha and Luna. They bowed politely as I turned and walked toward the stage. Time for the speech.

Emery

For a moment, all eyes were on me. Then, as quickly as the attention came, it faded, and people went back to their conversations.

But *his* eyes… I felt them instantly. I sighed with relief when I realized he hadn't fully recognized me yet.

I drifted along the edges of the hall, avoiding crowds. Then I froze. My old pack.

Thankfully, they hadn't seen me. I noticed Dexter speaking with them before he stepped away and mounted the stage. My pulse quickened. This was going to be… interesting. I slipped behind a couple, hiding in their shadow.

"Good evening, ladies and gentlemen, especially the ladies." *Laughter erupted.*

"Is everyone having a good time?" *Murmurs of agreement spread across the hall.* "Good, good. I'm glad.

"Before the fun begins, I would like to take this moment to express my condolences to the Tres Moon Pack, who have recently lost their beloved son. I'm sure we all heard the news, am I correct?" *More confirmations around the room.*

"I have a special gift for the Pack tonight. We have found the killer. And in fact… the killer is in this very room.

"They will be given the chance to step forward and reveal themselves. If not… we will do it for them. This is your one and only chance."
His voice was stern, unwavering.

A wave of gasps spread through the crowd. Guests turned on each other, whispering, staring, suspicion thick in the air.
Damn.

CHAPTER 13:

Emery

People kept glancing at one another, fear in their eyes, no doubt wondering if the killer might strike again.

I smirked. *Might as well get this over with. Here goes nothing.*
I began walking. My heels clicked with each step, drawing attention. Heads turned toward the sound. By the time I stepped into the middle of the banquet hall floor, every eye was on me. Some gasped, but most stayed silent.

"Emery?" Dexter was the first to speak, his voice faltering as if he couldn't believe what he was seeing. "What are you doing here?"

I chuckled. "Well, I have an invitation. Naturally, I came to the party."
I held up the letter, the one I'd made sure to retrieve from the guard at the door.
"How? You're a human," his right-hand man, Jeff, I think, said.
"Well, well. I never claimed to be human or not. *You* all assumed it."
I smirked.

"Why are you here, then?" Dexter asked.

I looked at him, smiling. Then realization hit him. He shook his head.
"Please… tell me it's not true?" he pleaded, desperation in his voice.
"Well. I can't. Because it *is* true. Honestly, I'm surprised it took this long. Oh, poor little Emery, could never hurt anyone…" I laughed sadistically, letting my eyes settle on the Alpha and Luna of my old pack.

"How could you?!" they both shouted.

The hall was silent except for their cries. Dexter stepped closer, his men flanking him. I took a small step back, not from fear, but from the sadness I saw in his eyes. It pierced me like an arrow straight to the heart. I masked it quickly, hiding my pain behind a villain's smile.

I scoffed and rolled my eyes. "Oh, please. As if you didn't know. Your son should've rejected me the moment he realized I was his mate. But no… he kept me for *your* sake. And all the while, you sat there knowing he fooled around behind my back. Pain, every single day. So… I got rid of him, for my own sake." I grinned wickedly. "That just proves you should never underestimate anyone. He had it coming, him and his bitch. I played the innocent girl and fooled everyone… even your precious Prince." I turned to Dexter. He looked utterly baffled.

"That is ENOUGH!" His voice boomed, fury and grief colliding. "You fooled us all, indeed. But you know the laws of the Moon Packs. Actions have consequences, and yours is a grave one. I hope you understand." His eyes burned into mine. "Before we begin your punishment, do you have anything to say?"

I glanced around the hall, emotions crashing over me in waves. Maybe I hadn't fully realized what I'd done… or what awaited me. But when my eyes met the man I had begun to love, sadness consumed me. For a brief flicker, it showed. Then I smothered it beneath a smile.

"Do your worst," I said simply.

Gasps rippled through the room. No one expected me to say that.

I knew what awaited me. I'd chosen my path long ago, and the ending would always be the same. But at least I'd die knowing I'd been loved, even if only for a short time.

"Very well then," Dexter declared, his voice heavy with both authority and sorrow. "I, Prince Dexter, hereby sentence Emerald of Tres Moon Pack, for the murder of Chase of Tres Moon Pack, to death. Carry out the order."
Jeff raised his weapon. I closed my eyes.

Gunshot.

The sound echoed through the hall. My body crumpled to the floor.
"I hope this brings you peace," Dexter said quietly to Alpha Eric. He nodded; grief etched into his face.

I crouched beside Emerald's still form, fingers to her neck, no pulse. Just as my heart had stopped with her.

Standing tall again, I commanded, "Take her body and clean this up."
The evening ended in chaos, the hall clearing as I dismissed everyone.

Emery
Closing my eyes, I heard the trigger cock, my breathing quickened, and then… nothing.

Darkness swallowed me whole.

The End.
…Or is it the end?

EPILOGUE

Narrator's POV

The end is not truly the end for Emerald. She is the chosen one of the Moon Goddess herself. Her tasks were simple, and she completed them… though the price was her life.

But what of our Prince? Let us see how he fares…

9 781967 086290